A Just Right Book

SALLY WANTS TO HELP

By Cindy Wheeler

Random House New York

Mommy has work to do. Sally wants to help.

The telephone rings.

Mommy talks and talks.

"Help! Help!"

Mommy helps Sally get untangled.

Here are some toys for Sally.

But Sally wants to help Mommy.

Mommy is busy now. Would Sally like a carrot?

Sally is busy too. Would Kitty like a carrot?

"Sally carry basket too?"

Mommy loves Sally.

But Mommy has work to do.

"Pretty day," says Sally.

"Kitty's outside!"

"Sally help Mommy work outside?"

What a good idea!

Library of Congress Cataloging-in-Publication Data:
Wheeler, Cindy. Sally wants to help. (A Just right book) SUMMARY: Mommy finds it hard to get her work done when baby Sally insists on helping her.
[1. Babies—Fiction. 2. Parent and child—Fiction] I. Title. II. Series. PZ7.W5593Sal 1988 [E] 88-3152 ISBN: 0-394-89339-5

Manufactured in Singapore 1 2 3 4 5 6 7 8 9 0   JUST RIGHT BOOKS is a trademark of Random House, Inc.